MISHA
DISAPPEARS

Misha had escaped.
Ben looked for his rabbit
inside the wooden hutch.
He looked for Misha around the yard
and under the bushes.
He looked at the back gate –
it was open.
"Mom," he shouted.
"Misha's gone!"

Mrs. Keene looked out the door,
with her coffee in her hand.
"Oh dear," she said.
"It must have been the repairman, Ben.
He came to fix the garage door,
and he went through the back gate."

Ben groaned.
Why had he gone for a ride on his bike...
why had he left Misha
out in the yard...
why hadn't he put her back
in her hutch before going out?

Ben thought of Misha hopping happily
down Hill Street.
He thought of savage dogs chasing her.
He thought of speeding cars squashing her.
He thought of Misha all alone and frightened.
Ben was sure he would never see Misha again.

Everyone on Hill Street
joined in the search for Misha.
Stuart rode up and down on his skateboard
and asked if anyone had seen
a brown and white rabbit.

Amanda and her grandma looked
under the shrubs and bushes.
Misha did not jump out to greet them.

Mrs. Jennings put up a sign
in her shop saying

Nobody found Misha.

Ben lay on the grass beside the rabbit hutch
and watched the sun disappear.
He watched the moon slide into the sky
and make shadows across the yard.
Even the shadows seemed sad and lonely.
Ben listened to the loud music
from the house next door.
People were laughing and singing.
How could anyone be happy tonight...
how could he ever be happy again?

13

"Come for dinner, Ben," called his mother.
Ben was too miserable to eat anything.

"Come and play cards, Ben," suggested his father.
Ben was too unhappy to play cards either.

That night when he climbed into bed,
he could not sleep.

The next day, Ben forgot his school lunch.
He forgot his shoes for gym,
and he forgot to go to his music lesson
after school.

But he could not forget about poor Misha.

Ben walked sadly home from school in the rain.
He ran up the driveway to his front door,
calling, "Mom…MOM…has anyone found Misha?"

Mrs. Keene opened the front door calmly.
"Oh hello, darling.
Just go out and bring in the washing for me,
will you?"

Ben didn't care if the washing got wet.
His mother didn't seem to care about Misha
anymore.
Had she forgotten already?

Ben tugged the clothes from the line.
The clothespins flew off in all directions,
and one landed right on top of Misha's hutch.

PLOP!
Ben saw a tiny flash of brown and white
inside the cage.
Poor Misha, he thought.
She always got a fright
when the clothespins thumped
on top of her hutch like that.

MISHA...
Ben dropped the clothes on the wet grass.
MISHA...
Ben reached the hutch
in one enormous leap.
MISHA WAS BACK!

Ben's mother stood on the doorstep, laughing.
"Guess where she was, Ben!" she called.
"Misha was in the garage.
She must have hopped inside
when the repairman was fixing the door.
Dad found her there this morning –
very dusty and very hungry, but very happy."

Ben hugged Misha tightly.
He thought of his terrible fears.
He thought of how miserable he had been,
and he thought of the dinner
he had missed last night.

Misha's soft nose tickled Ben's neck
as if to say sorry
for all the trouble she'd caused.

"You're forgiven," said Ben,
stroking Misha's soft head,
"and I'll be more careful of you
in the future."
Ben smiled happily at his mother and said,
"Now could I have something to eat, please?"